NIMOSHOM

AND HIS BUS

Penny M. Thomas

Karen Hibbard

HIGHWATER PRESS

For "Mush" Carl Bird.

— **P.T.**

To Hilde & Fred: Thanks for reading
to me when I was little!

— **K.H.**

Nimoshom drove a school bus. Sometimes he spoke in Cree.

Nimoshom means **my grandfather** in Cree.

In the morning, nimoshom would greet the kids. He would say:

"**Tansi!**" **Tansi** means **hello**.

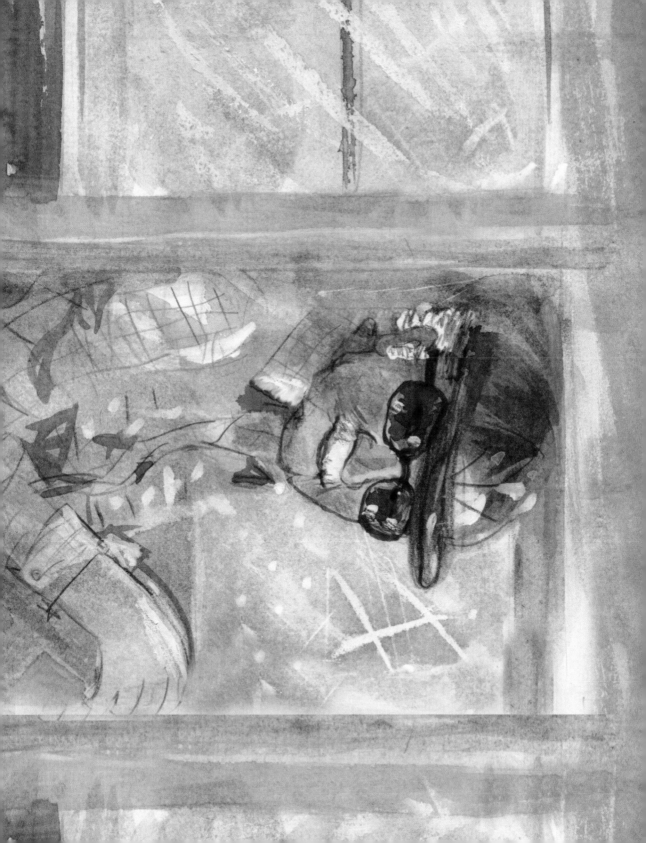

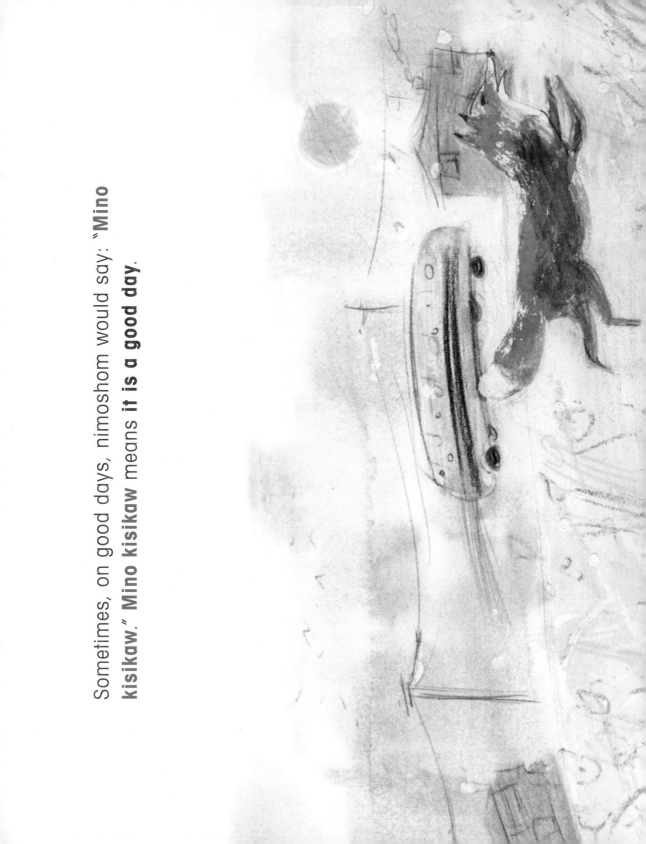

Sometimes, on good days, nimoshom would say: "Mino kisikaw." **Mino kisikaw** means **it is a good day**.

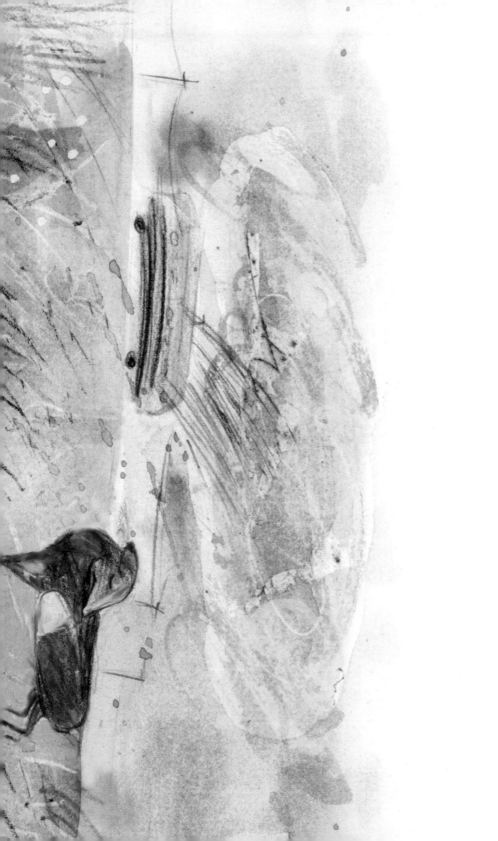

If it was a stormy day he would tell the kids: "**Machi kisikaw.**"
Machi kisikaw means **it is a bad day**.

When kids played around on the bus, nimoshom would say:
"Api!" **Api** means **sit down**.

Some mornings, the kids were running late, and nimoshom would tell them to **hurry up** coming to the bus. He would say: "**Kinapi!**" **Kinapi** means **hurry up**.

All the kids liked nimoshom. Nimoshom had the best smile. At Christmas, they brought him presents. It always made his day. He would smile and say: "**Ekosani**." **Ekosani** means **thank you**.

The kids always talked to nimoshom when he drove the bus. They would ask if he was having a good day. He always said: "**Ehe**." **Ehe** means **yes**. Sometimes they would ask him to drive faster. He would always laugh and say: "**Mots**." **Mots** means **no**.

If nimoshom was on the CB radio, and kids were trying to get his attention, he would kindly tell them: "**Cheskwa.**" **Cheskwa** means **wait**. He always talked to them when he was finished, though. He would say: "**Kekwan?**" **Kekwan** means **what**.

When little kids first came on the bus, nimoshom would let them sit in the front. He would tell them silly stories. He would look at them seriously and say: "**Tapwe!**" **Tapwe** means **truly**. He liked to tease with his silly stories.

Some Cree people don't say goodbye. Nimoshom was one of them. Instead, at the end of the day when he dropped off the kids, he said: "**Ekosi**." **Ekosi** has many meanings. It means **okay, that's it**, or **amen**.

Nimoshom was a good man. **Ekosi.**

CREE WORD LIST

Api: sit down

Cheskwa: wait

Ehe: yes

Ekosani: thank you

Ekosi: okay, that's it, amen

Kekwan: what

Kinapi: hurry up

Machi kisikaw: it is a bad day

Mino kisikaw: it is a good day

Mots: no

Nimoshom: my grandfather

Tansi: hello

Tapwe: truly

HighWater Press gratefully acknowledges the financial support of the Province of Manitoba through the Department of Culture, Heritage & Tourism and the Manitoba Book Publishing Tax Credit, and the Government of Canada through the Canada Book Fund (CBF) for our publishing activities.

The publisher also acknowledges the support of the Canada Council for the Arts, which last year invested $153 million to bring the arts to Canadians throughout the country.

Nous remercions le Conseil des arts du Canada de son soutien. L'an dernier, le Conseil a investi 153 millions de dollars pour mettre de l'art dans la vie des Canadiennes et des Canadiens de tout le pays.

Canada Council   Conseil des arts
for the Arts   du Canada

Printed and bound in Canada by Friesens
Design by Relish New Brand Experience
24 23 22 21 20 19 18 17   1 2 3 4 5

Library and Archives Canada Cataloguing in Publication

Thomas, Penny, 1979-, author
    Nimoshom and his bus / Penny M. Thomas ; [illustrations by]
Karen Hibbard.

Text in English; includes some text in Cree.
ISBN 978-1-55379-708-1 (hardcover)

PS8639 H585 T46 2017   jC813'.6   C2017-902716-6
ebook(ePub) 978-1-55379-733-3 ebook(PDF) 978-1-55379-734-0

ISBN 978-1-55379-708-1 (hardcover)

I. Title.

www.highwaterpress.com
Toll-free: 1-800-667-9673

HIGHWATER
PRESS